A Creature Was Stirring

For Mom and Dad, with love – C.G.

**SIMON AND
SCHUSTER**

First published
in Great Britain in
2006 by Simon & Schuster
UK Ltd, Africa House,
64-78 Kingsway, London WC2B 6AH

This paperback edition first published in 2007

Originally published in 2006 by Simon & Schuster Books

for Young Readers an imprint of Simon & Schuster

Children's Publishing Division, New York. Text and illustrations copyright

© 2006 Carter Goodrich. The right of Carter Goodrich to be identified as the author

and illustrator of this work has been asserted by him in accordance with the Copyright,

Designs and Patents Act, 1988. The illustrations for this book are rendered in

coloured pencils and watercolour. All rights reserved, including the right of reproduction in whole

or in part in any form. A CIP catalogue record for this book is available from the

British Library upon request

ISBN-10: 1-8473-8096-4

ISBN-13: 978-1-8473-8096-8

Printed in China

1 3 5 7 9 10 8 6 4 2

A Creature Was Stirring

By Clement C. Moore and Carter Goodrich
Illustrated by Carter Goodrich

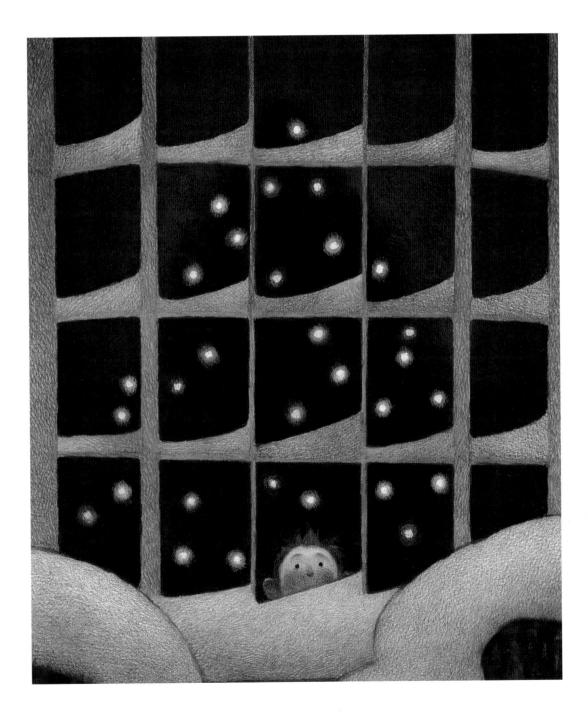

SIMON & SCHUSTER
New York   London   Sydney

You all know this tale,
But read this, you'll see:
One creature was stirring,
That creature was me!

'Twas the night before Christmas, when all through the house
Not a creature was stirring, not even a mouse.
The stockings were hung by the chimney with care,
In hopes that St Nicholas soon would be there.

I don't want to butt in,
But I'm wide awake,
And in Santa's book
That's a naughty mistake.

The children were nestled all snug in their beds,
While visions of sugar-plums danced in their heads.
And Mama in her kerchief, and I in my cap,
Had just settled our brains for a long winter's nap.

How can they sleep?
I do wish I could.
He'll write in that book;
He'll write I'm no good!

When out on the lawn there arose such a clatter,
I sprang from the bed to see what was the matter.
Away to the window I flew like a flash,
Tore open the shutters and threw up the sash.

He's here! I can hear him!
Now what do I do?
Don't panic, don't move...
Look fast asleep, too!

The moon on the breast of the new-fallen snow
Gave the lustre of midday to objects below,
When, what to my wondering eyes should appear,
But a miniature sleigh and eight tiny reindeer.

I might as well look
To be sure that he's real,
My friend says he's not,
But that's not how I feel.

With a little old driver, so lively and quick,
I knew in a moment it must be St Nick.
More rapid than eagles, his coursers they came,
And he whistled and shouted, and called them by name.

Oh wow, there he is!
And I'm in it for now.
I've been naughty twice;
To look's not allowed.

"Now, Dasher! Now, Dancer! Now, Prancer and Vixen!
On, Comet! On, Cupid! On, Donner and Blitzen!
To the top of the porch! To the top of the wall!
Now dash away! Dash away! Dash away, all!"

They're coming up now!
They're moving this way!
St Nicholas, toys,
Reindeer and sleigh!

As dry leaves that before the wild hurricane fly,
When they meet with an obstacle, mount to the sky,
So up to the house-top the coursers they flew,
With a sleigh full of toys, and St Nicholas too.

Okay, try to calm down
And climb back in bed,
Don't look like your breathing...
Pretend that you're dead!

And then, in a twinkling, I heard on the roof
The prancing and pawing of each little hoof.
As I drew in my head, and was turning around,
Down the chimney St Nicholas came with a bound.

He's landed above!
His sleigh's just outside!
Wow, look at that thing,
What a fabulous ride!

He was dressed all in fur, from his head to his foot,
And his clothes were all tarnished with ashes and soot.
A bundle of toys he had flung on his back,
And he looked like a peddler just opening his pack.

That sleigh is still moving
If I'm not mistaken…
Didn't he put
The sleigh parking brake on?

His eyes, how they twinkled! His dimples, how merry!
His cheeks were like roses, his nose like a cherry!
His droll little mouth was drawn up like a bow,
And the beard of his chin was as white as the snow.

Oh, what was that rhyme?
That command they all knew?
He shouted it once
And this thing really flew.

The stump of a pipe he held tight in his teeth,
And the smoke it encircled his head like a wreath.
He had a broad face and a little round belly,
That shook when he laughed, like a bowl full of jelly.

Come on, Dasher! Go, Comet!
Do something, Cupid!
That's it, dash away!
(Gosh, I feel rather stupid.)

He was chubby and plump, a right jolly old elf,
And I laughed when I saw him, in spite of myself.
A wink of his eye and a twist of his head
Soon gave me to know I had nothing to dread.

Okay, easy does it,
Just put her down nice.
If he catches me now,
He'll write "naughty" thrice.

He spoke not a word, but went straight to his work,
And filled all the stockings, then turned with a jerk,
And laying his finger aside of his nose,
And giving a nod, up the chimney he rose.

Quick! Back inside!
Now, reindeer, you STAY!
That thing's safely parked;
Let's keep it that way.

He sprang to his sleigh, to his team gave a whistle,
And away they all flew like the down of a thistle.
But I heard him exclaim, 'ere he drove out of sight,

"HAPPY CHRISTMAS TO ALL
and to all a good night!"